Princess
Paige

PRINCESS FOR PRESIDENT

By Stacey Solt

ISBN: 9798551663393

Books by Stacey Solt

The Princess Paige series

A Royal Discovery

Princess for President

Queen of Hearts

Summer School

Contents

1. The Announcement

My name is Paige Johnson. I am in fourth grade at Riverview Elementary School.

I grew up in Riverview with my mom, dad, sister and brother. I had a normal life until last month, when I discovered that I'm a princess!

My grandfather moved to America when he was two years old. He was born Prince Richard Albertus-Gianna of Altura, but never knew that he was born into a royal family.

Even though I'm a princess now, not much has changed. I still go to school with my friends.

My mom tells me to load the dishwasher. And my teachers still make me do homework.

Even princesses have to do math homework.

Halloween is this week. Our teacher, Mrs. Henry, throws the best Halloween parties in the school. My friends have decided to dress up as princesses for this year's party. We're going trick-or-treating together.

This week is exciting for another reason. Our art teacher is finally back at school. She had a baby this summer and this is her first week back.

Because today is a Monday, we won't have art for a few days. Our class has computer class on Mondays. It's a lot of fun, but I wish we had art every day of the week.

We start our day with the morning announcements. Our principal wishes a boy in second grade a happy birthday. I wish my birthday was this close to Halloween. I could have a costume party! Instead, I'm stuck with a

February birthday. Maybe we'll have a Valentine's Day theme this year.

I'm so busy planning my birthday party that I almost miss Principal Andrew's next announcement.

"Don't forget that this week starts our school election cycle!" he says, his voice booming out of the speaker above our desks. "Every person running for student government must submit their name to me by the end of this week. You'll have this week and next week to campaign and convince your classmates to vote for you."

"Our school's election will be held next Friday," he adds. "That's just a few days after your parents vote in this year's presidential election!"

As the loudspeaker goes silent, Jay McNeil walks into the room. Jay moved to our school last year and one of the quietest kids in our class.

Mrs. Henry smiles at him but shakes her head,

pointing to the door. If you're late for homeroom, you have to go back to the office for a late pass. Then she walks to the front of the room with a stack of forms and hands one to each of us.

"Like Mr. Andrew said, our school election starts this week. This paper describes the student government's jobs and how the election works. There can only be one fourth grade president, but we'll also need a vice-president to help the president, and a treasurer and secretary."

I read over the sheet. The treasurer is in charge of field trip money, which could be fun. They organize fundraisers and help plan our big trip at the end of the year. The secretary takes notes during class meetings, and makes sure the meetings run smoothly.

The class president and vice-president meet with the teachers and principal every month. They share what kids in our grade are concerned about, and try to find ways to solve problems in the school.

My mind wanders off to a conversation I had with Prince Alex, my cousin, just a few weeks ago. *"I will never be the king of Altura, but I still plan to do a lot of good in this world. You can also do great things,"* he told me. *"Find ways to make changes for the better, first at your school and then in your town. Small changes can lead to big things."*

This could be my chance to make a difference! I could work with the teachers to make our school a better place. First I'd help my school, then my town, and then maybe the world! This seems like a great step for a new princess.

As I read the bottom of the form, which describes how we can run for office, Lucas Bates stands up and clears his throat.

"Mrs. Henry, I'm gonna run for class president!" he says. "Kids in our grade work way too hard. We need less homework and more ice cream. Vote for me next week!"

A few girls behind Lucas giggle quietly. He turns around to glare at them.

"What, you don't like ice cream?" he asks. "You'll see. I'll make a great president!"

I sigh and lean towards Emily Ellis's desk. "Em, do you want to run with me? Would you be my vice president if I ran for president? We can't let Lucas win."

She leans towards me with a big smile. "Let's do it," she says, raising her hand and waiting for Mrs. Henry to call on her.

"Paige and I will also be running for president and vice president," she says, sounding very professional. "We'll announce our campaign goals soon. Please let us know what changes you'd like to see in our school!"

Emily is really smart. Instead of announcing what she wants to do, she's asking the whole class what they'd like to happen. I just hope enough kids don't vote for free ice cream.

We fill out our election forms and turn them in. A few other kids in our class turn in their own forms. Logan Gray says he wants to be treasurer, and Max Coleman is running for secretary.

Then it's time to walk to the computer lab for our weekly typing race. There are hot air balloons for each class on the front board, moving higher each week to count how many words we've typed. The class that types the most words this marking period wins a pizza party.

Mrs. Henry's class is in second place now. I work extra hard to help our class balloon move higher. I like to work hard, and I like to win!

I'm tired by the time I get home. It's been a long day. My mind is filled with ideas for the class election.

Mom is in the kitchen chopping tomatoes and lettuce, her curly brown hair pulled back into a messy bun. I grab a banana and sit to watch her work. Mom is a nurse and worked the entire weekend at the hospital. She doesn't work today, and she always cooks a family meal on her days off.

"How was school today?" she asks.

"It was great!" I say. "We had spaghetti for lunch today, and Emma shared her garlic bread. We're in first place in our typing race again. And I'm running for class president!"

I finish eating my banana, and walk across the kitchen to throw the peel into our compost bin.

Mom smiles and puts down the vegetables she's chopping. She holds out an apron for me.

"Wow. That was a busy day! Tell me about running for class president. Are you having a real election? And do you think this is enough tomatoes for our tacos?"

She points to a small mountain of chopped tomatoes on her cutting board. My brother and I love tomatoes. I tie on my apron, then grab two more tomatoes and start washing them at the sink.

I tell her about the election in two weeks, and that Lucas is also running for president. I know Emily and I can do a good job, but who doesn't love free ice cream?

"Free ice cream and less homework is hard to beat," my mom agrees. "Are you sure the teachers would agree to these things? You need goals that the students like, but the teachers have to like them, too."

"When's the last time you called Prince Alexander?" she asks. "He should have some good advice. Call him before supper and tell him you're running for class president."

That's a great idea! I'm sure he will know what to do.

Prince Alexander (who has asked Mom to call him Alex at least a hundred times) is my royal cousin who lives in America. He owns his own business, working with schools that need computers and internet access or other things to learn.

I take off my apron, give Mom a kiss, and run to my room to call Alex. After six rings it goes to his voicemail. He's a busy person.

"Hi, Alex!" I say. "It's Paige. I'm running for class president, and I need your advice! Please call me back."

I hang up, then stare at the phone for a few minutes. Once I'm sure that he won't call back right away, I sigh and go back downstairs. Maybe Mom will make garlic bread with our tacos.

2. Chaos in the Classroom

It's Tuesday. Gym class.

The morning goes quickly. There are a few morning announcements. The principal wishes a few more kids "happy birthday," and also reminds us about the school's Halloween party on Friday.

Every year, when the town hosts trick-or-treat night, our school has a Halloween party. There are games and prizes in the gym. We can trick-or-treat between classrooms, too.

Some of the teachers give out treats like

pumpkin-shaped erasers, but our principal gives big candy bars to the best-dressed kids. I can't wait to see Mrs. Henry at the party. She always has a great costume.

The announcements end while I'm still thinking about Halloween. Our class marches down the stairs, past the library and kindergarten classrooms. Every door is closed and full of students, except for one. The door leading to the art room is open and I can hear our art teacher, Mrs. Palette, talking inside.

As I've said before, art is my favorite class. It's so much fun to create new things. We just finished painting portraits of ourselves! I can't wait to see what projects we start this week. I glance inside the classroom as we walk by, hoping for clues.

Instead of clues, I see chaos. The art room is a complete mess. I stop walking and Jay bumps into me. Emily and Max bump into both of us.

We make a big traffic jam, but it's not nearly as messy as what I see in the art room.

Macaroni is everywhere. It covers the floor and chairs, like someone's opened a few boxes and danced around while holding them. An empty pasta box sits on the floor with its top ripped off.

That's not the worst of it, though. There's paint everywhere! Rivers of paint are running along the biggest table. The shelves above the table are filled with knocked-over paint bottles, flooding the table and floor with a rainbow of colors. All of our beautiful paint is ruined.

Mrs. Palette stands in the middle of the room, holding a broom and slowly sweeping up the macaroni on the floor. She looks stunned.

I rush into the classroom with Emily. The rest of our class crowds around the doorway to get a better look.

"Paige! Emily! What are you doing?" Mrs.

Henry asks. "Please get back in line!"

She stops talking and moves around us, stepping into the art room.

"Whoa! What happened here?" Mrs. Henry says.

Mrs. Palette turns, and seems surprised to see all of us watching her. "I'm not sure what happened," she says. "The room was a mess when I got here a few minutes ago. Someone dumped all of my supplies on the floor! I just talked to the principal, and he says none of the other classrooms were destroyed."

She brushes the hair out of her face and sighs. "It's my first week back! Who would do this? They've ruined everything we need for this week's project."

My heart sinks as I look at the paint dripping off the shelves. I was really looking forward to this week's art lesson. It's also not fair that Mrs. Palette has to clean up this huge mess.

I step past Mrs. Henry and put my hand on Mrs. Palette's arm.

"It's OK," I say. "We can help you clean this up. And I have a ton of paint and supplies at home if you need them. I'm sure other kids would want to help, too!"

Mrs. Palette gives a little laugh, and one tear runs down her cheek. "Thank you, Paige. I have paint I can bring into school too, but I appreciate your offer. It's very sweet."

I pick up a dustpan and start cleaning pasta off the chairs. Emily finds some paper towels and starts picking up overturned paint bottles, carefully wiping the paint off each one.

After a few minutes, the room looks much cleaner. It's amazing how much you can get done if you work together.

I hear a noise in the hallway and look up. Mrs. Henry is standing there, but the rest of our class is gone. She gestures for us to come into the hallway. Emily and I put down our cleaning supplies and walk out of the art room.

"It was nice of you to help Mrs. Palette, but it's time to get back to class," she says. "The custodian will be here in a few minutes. He'll help clean up the rest of the mess."

Mrs. Palette comes out to give us both a hug, and promises to be ready for our class later this week. She even hints that she'll make a trip to the grocery store tonight. It sounds like the pasta boxes were a big part of this week's project.

We walk towards the back doors with Mrs. Henry. She tells us that since gym class has already started, the rest of our class is outside playing soccer. Emily looks excited. She loves when we have gym class outside.

I'm not excited at all. Who can think about soccer when someone is destroying the art room? I promise myself that I'll help Mrs. Palette discover who made this mess.

3. Royal Ambitions

I'm finishing my homework that night when the phone rings in the kitchen. I let my big sister answer it. My friends never call after dinner, because they're busy with their own homework.

I'm surprised when Ashley knocks on my bedroom door and comes in holding the phone.

"It's for you. Prince Alex is calling you back," she says.

I grin and reach for the phone.

When I ask Alex how he's doing, he says he's been busy. His company delivered more than 500 laptops to an elementary school yesterday! He thinks all kids should have access to technology and new ways of learning. His company raises money to donate laptops, tablets and other supplies to schools that need them.

I look at my desk. My laptop is open while I finish my homework. My sister and I don't even have to share computers, because Dad says we need them for school. We're really lucky.

I want to be like Alex and help kids, too.

When Alex asks why I called, I keep staring at my laptop.

"I want to run for class president. But I'm also sad, because I thought that being a princess would change me. Nothing's changed," I say. "I go to school, come home, and do my homework. When will I get to do something important and help people?"

Tears start leaking out of my eyes. I wipe them away and take a deep breath.

"Can I work for your company?" I ask. "If I become class president, our whole school can help you!"

Alex laughs. "While I would love to work with you, your first project needs to be something you love. It needs to shout 'Paige did this!'" he says. "When I started raising money to get computers into schools, I didn't have a company. I was working alone. But it was something that I thought was important. One passionate person can make a big difference, even if they start small."

Then Alex asks me what I am passionate about. What do I love doing?

"Art!" I say immediately. "I love doing art. Even when we don't have school or art class, I'm still drawing or painting or even playing with modeling clay."

"That's great! Let's figure out how you could use art to help people. Why do you love art so much?" he asks.

I pause, looking at the drawing pencils I have lined up on my desk. Before I started my homework, I was going through supplies and finding things I could give to Mrs. Palette.

I've never thought about why I do art. I just love creating things.

"Well, I like getting caught up in a big project," I say slowly, thinking over my answer. "It makes me stop thinking about my problems. Sometimes it even helps me come up with answers to those problems, even when I'm not really thinking about them. Pretty strange, right? Like if I have a big science project to work on, sometimes doodling helps me come up with ways to make my project better."

"That's not strange at all," says Alex. "Hey, did you know that some schools are starting to use art in regular lessons? Drawing is all about proportions, which means you have to be good at math. If you don't understand how to divide a person's face into equal portions, the face you draw is going to look funny."

He starts to speak more quickly, sounding excited. "Art can help kids learn in other ways, too! Kids who wouldn't normally read a book might like graphic novels. They can split up into small groups to draw and write a graphic novel, which takes a lot of reading and art skills."

Sign me up! I'd love going to a school that uses art every day.

This reminds me of Mrs. Henry's monthly projects. Our class does big projects like creating a business plan (her chocolate sale was so yummy) or researching their family's history to help everyone learn new things. What if she used new art projects each month instead?

I start to wonder where the nearest elementary art school is, and if my parents could drive me there every day. I'm pretty sure there isn't one close enough to take the school bus.

I pace across the room as Alex starts talking about his company's new coding program. Now that so many schools in his area have computers and the basic technology they need, he's working on expanding how each school uses those computers. One of their newest programs lets kids create their own drawings and animations, using numbers and code instead of a pencil and paper. It's another new way to combine technology and learning.

Only half listening, I stop pacing and walk to my computer to search for art schools. The nearest school I can find is almost an hour away! Would Mom and Dad let me live away from home if the school was too far? Dad has some cousins across the state.

My brother Franky starts kindergarten next year, though. I'd miss him if I wasn't living at home. He's also really excited to go to school with me.

It's so unfair that we can't have art schools like this closer to home.

Then it clicks. I step back from the computer to grab the phone with both hands.

"That's how I can make our school better!" I say. "I don't have to find a really cool art school somewhere else. If I was class president, I could work with the teachers and bring art into every class in our own school!"

"That's the spirit!" Alex says. "Find your passion. Once you do that, you can't help but make the world a better place."

We start to outline some ideas, from bringing Alex's coding program into my school to a book challenge that gets students reading, writing and creating books for the rest of the school to enjoy.

Alex promises to send me more information about his company's coding program, as well as the research he's read about schools using art throughout the school day.

Next, we talk about my campaign strategy. "Campaign" is a fancy word to describe how I'll get people to vote for me. Alex says that it's not enough to have great ideas. You have to share those ideas with the whole school.

It's important for Mrs. Henry's class to know why I'd make the best class president, but I also need to convince the hundreds of kids in my grade who aren't in my class. Every vote counts!

Because I'm running a campaign to combine art and learning, we agree that I'll need some really cool, hand-drawn campaign posters. I even come up with the idea of recruiting some of my gymnastics and dance friends. The visual arts can be a fun way to learn, too.

After an hour of talking, Alex says that he needs to get off the phone.

"I need to finish some work tonight, but you're off to a great start," he says. "I'm glad to see you excited about this!"

This calls for an art break. I hang up the phone and start sketching some poster ideas.

If I become president, I promise to be kind and fair, and bring art into the classroom every day. That has to be better than free ice cream.

4. Farm Day

The next day is Farm Day. Fourth grade is spending the morning at a local animal farm. There's even a pumpkin patch and hay rides.

Our class goes into the pumpkin patch first. We climb into a wagon filled with hay bales, laughing and talking as we take the long, bumpy road to the pumpkin patch.

Mrs. Henry tells us that we're each allowed to pick one small pumpkin or gourd. I grab Emily's hand and pull her towards a field filled with tiny pink and red pumpkins. They're adorable! My mom would love to have a pink pumpkin.

Once we've each picked a pumpkin, we climb into the wagon to ride back to the main farm. While other classes are in the pumpkin patch, we'll be meeting the farm owner and walking through his petting zoo.

Standing outside of the zoo's gates is a young man wearing jeans and a long-sleeve flannel shirt.

"Good morning, boys and girls! I'm Mr. Tanner," he says. "Welcome to our family's farm! We're going into the petting zoo next, but there are a few rules. Be kind to the animals. No hurting them or teasing them with food. Take turns petting the animals. We don't want to scare or overwhelm them. But most importantly, I want you to have fun and learn something! Whenever you drink milk, or eat a hamburger, or even eat a bowl of cereal, don't forget that your food came from a farmer. Come on, let's look around."

He walks us quickly through the zoo, pointing out the cow milking station and encouraging us to try milking a cow once our tour is over.

Next he stops at the sheep pen. Mr. Tanner tells us that his sheep aren't raised for meat, but he does sell their wool to a person who makes yarn. Their wool is sheared in spring to keep the sheep cool in the summer. That wool is used to make sweaters and other clothes to keep people warm in the winter!

Finally he stops at a fenced-in area filled with goats and some climbing areas.

"You can pet our sheep, but the goats are our friendliest animals," he says. "They love to play around, and they also like to eat food right out of your hands! Just take a small handful of corn, or some hay, and the goats will come right up to you."

He sticks his hand into the canvas bag filled with corn, then sighs when corn starts pouring out the bottom of the bag.

"Sorry about that, kids. Looks like the mice got to our corn first. They chewed a hole in the bag! Small animals like mice will eat whatever food they can find, and destroy whatever stands between them and their food."

Mr. Tanner pulls the bag off its stand and promises to get us a fresh bag, then tells us to start exploring the zoo.

Emily and I walk with our friends and talk about the election. My friend Ella Fisher loves the idea of bringing art into the classroom. She promises to come over this weekend and help us with campaign posters.

I give her a big hug, then reach over to scratch the smallest goat behind his ears. He's cute. I've just scooped a handful of corn off the ground to feed him when Lucas walks over. He bumps me out of the way, then picks up the corn he knocked out of my hand.

"Watch what you're doing," he says. "You made a mess!"

I sigh and roll my eyes. I only made a mess because he bumped into me.

The goat eats all of the corn in his hand, but Lucas isn't ready to leave yet. He picks up a handful of hay and holds it over the fence. It's right outside of the goat's reach, even when the goat stands on its back legs. Lucas laughs as the goat tries to climb the fence.

"So if you're a princess, does that mean you have lots of little animal friends?" he asks. "Princesses love animals. It sounds like they make a mess, though."

He drops the hay onto the goat's face. I look around for the farmer. He's busy helping a few kids milk a cow across the field. Mrs. Henry is watching them and taking pictures. I wish they'd stop Lucas from teasing the goat. I wish I'd finally stand up to Lucas's teasing, too.

Then Lucas looks over at Ella and Emily.

"Are you guys going to dress like animals for Halloween? Paige needs some animal sidekicks. Or is Paige too good to play dress up now?" he asks.

Lucas and I have never been friends, but I can't believe how mean he's been lately. His words hurt like I've been punched in the stomach.

I never asked to be a princess. It's been fun getting to know my mom's family, but being a princess doesn't change who I am.

* * *

I'm quiet on the bus ride back to school. Do I really think I'm better than my friends?

No, of course I don't think that. I'm a good person and a good friend. I wish Lucas would stop making fun of me, because I can't change my family. I don't *want* to change my family. Alex is pretty awesome, and my mom has been so excited to learn about her family's history. She's even emailed her new cousins and wants to visit them soon.

When we're a few minutes away from the school, Mrs. Henry turns to face us from the front of the bus. She reminds us that there's still a few hours until school is over.

"Because a few of you are running for class office, I thought this would be a good time to talk about the election your parents will vote in next month!" she says.

Mrs. Henry looks excited. Even I get a little bit excited hearing this, and turn to grin at Emily. Maybe learning a few things about real elections will give us ideas.

We get back to school and settle into the classroom. Once we're all quiet, Mrs. Henry walks to the front of the room and draws three big circles on the white board.

"Our school election isn't quite the same as our country's election, but they are similar," she says. "The United States was created with a division of power. There are three 'branches' to the government, which means that one person is never in charge by themselves."

She writes down a few words in each circle:

Legislative (makes laws)
Executive (signs or vetoes laws)
Judicial (decides if laws follow Constitution)

"The legislative branch makes laws," she says. "There are 535 men and women in Congress. That's a lot of people trying to work together! But because our country is so large, people in different parts of the country usually want different things. Every one of our congressmen and women are trying to best represent their own state's needs."

She pauses, then asks those of us running for class office to raise our hands.

"Think of yourselves as the legislative branch," says Mrs. Henry. "You will listen to your classmates and decide what issues are most important. Do we need longer lunches? More gym class? Sharper pencils on test day? There are many different wants and needs among students. It will be your job to decide which problems are the most important, come up with possible solutions, and bring those ideas to your teachers."

She pointed to the next circle.

"The executive branch. That's me!" she says. "At least, that's the role your teachers and principal play in student government. We listen to the student government's ideas and decide if changes should be made. We can approve a change or veto it. If we 'veto' an idea, that means we stop it from happening."

Mrs. Henry adds that in the United States, the president and vice president are part of the executive branch. The president signs or vetoes laws passed by Congress. A law isn't official until it's signed by the president.

She points to the third circle, and notes that our school only has two "branches" of government – students and teachers. Our country has three branches.

"In the United States, we also have a third branch of government that watches over the others. The judicial branch includes the Supreme Court, which decides if laws are constitutional. Do they follow the basic rules we've established for our country, or does a law hurt our rights? The judicial branch only allows laws that follow our country's Constitution."

She puts down her marker and glances at the clock.

"Think of our school as a very small government," she says. "There are many different sizes of government, from federal lawmakers who create laws for the entire country, to state and local governments. Every size of government has an important job."

"It's almost time to pack up," she adds. "Students running for class office, don't forget to finalize your campaign ideas. Get those posters up in the hallway! Come to me with any questions! Let's get this election started."

5. Art Class

It's finally art day!

I've been waiting all week for our first lesson with Mrs. Palette. She's one of my favorite teachers. We had a great substitute while Mrs. Palette was home with her baby, but I'm glad she's back.

I'm also excited to tell Mrs. Palette about my ideas for the school. If I want to bring art into every classroom, I have to talk to the art teacher!

There's no time to talk to her this morning, though. Our bus gets to school late, and we walk through the front door as the first bell rings. Emily and I run down the hall to Mrs. Henry's room.

We rush around the corner and run right into Principal Andrew.

"Take it easy," he says, smiling at both of us. "I know you're both running for student government, but you can't *run* in the halls."

Mr. Andrew laughs at his own joke. "There's an assembly next week before all of the students vote. I can't wait to hear your campaign ideas," he adds. "Now get to class, but no more running!"

We walk down the hallway, careful not to run again.

Outside our classroom, I can hear Mrs. Henry talking to the class. Emily and I open our lockers and put away our coats and lunch boxes. It sounds like Mrs. Henry is reminding everyone about trick-or-treat tonight.

"Do you think we missed anything important?" Emily asks.

"Nope," I say. "The important things start in a few minutes. Let's hurry up. I don't want to miss art class!"

As I close my locker, the rest of our class lines up in the hallway. We dash to the back of the line to join them.

Mrs. Palette's room is much neater than it was earlier this week. There's no macaroni on the floor. Someone's cleaned up all of the spilled paint, too. It was a mess, but it did add a splash of color to the room.

Instead of going to my seat, I walk up to Mrs. Palette and give her a hug.

"I missed you!" I say. "Did you find out who made the mess in here?"

"I didn't, but hopefully it won't happen again," she says. "Sit down and we'll talk later. Let's make some art!"

This week's project will be food art. She's lined a long table with all of our favorite foods, from crackers and cookies to popcorn and four different kinds of pasta. We'll be using them to create works of art. So yummy!

Mrs. Palette starts by telling us that her favorite food is macaroni and cheese. She used macaroni and other shapes to make a pasta skeleton. It has a round rib cage, straight legs and arms made from spaghetti, and a bowtie noodle for its hips.

It even looks like it's dancing on the paper! She's drawn some music notes around its head. She's so creative. It's a great project for Halloween, too.

We line up and each take a bag filled with our favorite snack. I pick the pink princess crackers. Dad's been buying them ever since we found out our grandfather was a prince. Emily grabs the vanilla finger cookies.

The crackers are fish-shaped, so they should work perfectly. I take a blue piece of paper and carefully cut out the shape of a fish bowl. Then I glue the bowl onto a sturdy piece of white paper and attach a few crackers to my "bowl."

I draw a small underwater castle, then pause to look around at everyone else's work.

Wow! Emily used her finger cookies to make a palace. She's opened one cookie, and the icing looks like a white door leading into a golden palace. There's even a few towers with windows painted on them, and a vanilla Oreo sun.

I hear the sound of balls rolling across the table. As I look up, a dozen gum balls fall to the floor.

"Oh, man! This isn't working!" Jay says, scrambling to the floor to pick up the gum balls he's dropped. Instead of gathering them neatly, he scatters them across the room.

The three of us start chasing gum balls. Emily

stops one from rolling out the door. I find three hidden under the paint shelves. They're sticky with white glue and covered in pieces of broken pasta. Gross.

We bring them back to Jay, who puts the rest of the gum balls back into his bag.

"They won't stick!" he says. "I glued them twice. They just roll off."

Mrs. Palette comes over with a bottle of fast-drying glue. After she puts a dab of glue down for each gum ball, Jay pokes his project.

"Wow, it dried so fast! Thanks, Mrs. Palette!" he says.

As we start cleaning up, I ask Mrs. Palette if she has a minute to talk about my campaign ideas. She nods her head a few times, but seems concerned that there won't be enough time in the school day to make my plan work.

"Art is science, and math, and it helps to tell stories in literature, too. You've got some great ideas. But I'm only one person, and I already teach every student in this building," she says. "I love the concept, though. Let's keep thinking about how we could make it happen!"

We come up with a few ideas about how we could maximize her time and help our classroom teachers create their own art projects. We both agree that we'll have to start small, maybe with just a few classrooms.

By the time class is done and Mrs. Henry walks us back to her room, I'm more hopeful that my ideas could really happen. I'll put a lot of thought into this over the weekend.

But for now, there are just five hours until school is over. Then my friends and I can go home and transform ourselves into princesses. Trick-or-treat night is almost here!

6. Halloween

Emily rides the bus home with me that day. We'll need lots of room to get ready for trick-or-treat night, and Mom says we can use our basement. There's plenty of room for all of our friends.

My big sister Ashley answers the door. She sends each of our friends downstairs while I open snacks. Ashley tells us that she's too old for Halloween, but I think she's secretly jealous. We have amazing costumes this year.

Ashley is a princess, too. She's never announced it at school like I did, so only her best friends know. My brother told his entire preschool class that he was a prince. Alex visited his school, but they haven't made a big deal out of it.

Life as a princess has been pretty boring, to be honest. But I'm still going to have fun dressing up for Halloween.

I'm pouring one last bag of popcorn into a bowl when Emily tells me our friends are all here. Finally!

We both grab a bowl of snacks and head downstairs where Kendra Kelly, Hailey O'Connor, and Ella Fisher are waiting for us. The five of us have been good friends since kindergarten, even though Emily and I are the only two who have class together this year. I still see Hailey in gymnastics class, though.

The girls are carefully unpacking their costumes.

Ella has a bright yellow princess dress that she bought at the store. Even though yellow is her favorite color, I'm surprised by her choice. Her name is Isabella, but she hates being called Belle.

Kendra has bright red curly hair, so I'm not surprised to see her unpack a dark green Merida dress. She wore it last year. Kendra's always excited when she can reuse costumes.

Emily opens the basement closet door and pulls out our dresses. The other girls run over to and start examining them. We're so lucky! Emily's mom made princess gowns for both of us. They're not fancy, but she used layers of sparkly tulle to make them look like we're floating over the floor when we walk, just like real princesses.

Hailey feels my dress's light blue fabric and sighs.

"These dresses look amazing," she says. "The purple dress will be perfect for Emily, too. My mom wouldn't let me get a new dress for Halloween. All I have is my big sister's dress from the middle school dance."

She wrinkles her nose. I know how she feels. Borrowing special outfits from your sister is no fun.

"Paige is the real princess anyway," Hailey adds. "She needs a dress that looks amazing."

"No way," I say. "Tonight, we'll all be princesses! We'll all be beautiful. I just wanted to share some of the fun."

Kendra grins and reaches for her bag.

"We're going to look great. Look what I found!" she says, reaching for the bottom of the bag. She pulls out a handful of silver tiaras.

"We can't be dressed as princesses without a tiara! My little sister had these at her birthday party last month."

I put on the fake crown and walk over to the mirror, carefully adjusting it on my head. It's just what we needed.

"Thanks, Kendra!" I say. "They're perfect!"

We put on our dresses, and Ella helps each of us make our hair a bit fancy. Then we nibble on snacks while waiting for the sun to set. You can't go trick-or-treating when the sun is up!

We walk to a few houses in my neighborhood once it's properly dark outside.

All of the neighbors know that I'm a princess, of course. Dad was really excited to tell everyone what we discovered about Mom's family. Even though being a princess hasn't changed my life, I guess it is pretty exciting to find out that you married a princess – especially if you're a history teacher.

Still, I don't like it when the neighbors treat me differently. I'm glad that they greet all of my friends with a bright smile and lots of candy. Isn't Halloween great?

Once we're done, we pile into my parents' van. Dad drives us to the school.

"Look, it's Mr. Andrew!" Hailey shouts. "Is that a hover board?"

"It is!" Kendra says. "Look, he's floating and everything. But it looks like a flying carpet. Maybe he's Aladdin!"

We all giggle when we see his wife come out of the school dressed as Jasmine. She looks beautiful. I've never seen both of them in costume! Mrs. Andrew is the town's mayor, so she's usually dressed really nice.

Once Dad drops us off, we rush to the principal and mayor.

"Wonderful costumes, ladies," he says. "I hope you don't mind that Mrs. Andrew joined your princess theme."

We admire Mrs. Andrew's costume for a few minutes while the principal takes our photo with her. Then we head inside and go straight to the gym.

Inside the gym, long tables are set up against the wall. Each table is filled with treats, from candy and fruit to fun toys and handouts.

Our gym teacher even has a "jumping jack o' lanterns" station. A dozen kids are doing jumping jacks to earn a lollipop.

We can't do jumping jacks in our princess shoes. Instead, we stop at the reading teacher's table. Mrs. Williams has a "Reading is Wicked" sign hanging on the bleachers behind her, and gives us each a Riverview Elementary bookmark and a cookie from a jar that says "Warning: Real love spells baked into every bite."

Mmm. I love chocolate chip cookies. But I hope they don't make me fall in love!

We grab some caramel apples from the PTO table to eat while we look at the rest of the booths. The sticky, sweet caramel sticks to my teeth.

Lucas marches up to me and grabs the apple out of my hand. Taking a big bite out of the apple, he looks at each of our outfits and smirks. Then he grabs the tail hanging off his costume and holds it up so we can see it.

"Like my costume, Paige? I'm a mouse! Thought it would make your Cinderella costume look better."

I roll my eyes and don't answer him. Fortunately, the cookie's love spell isn't working. I could never fall in love with Lucas.

"I thought a mouse would work with your blue dress. You are dressed like Cinderella, right? Cinderella was a real princess, even though you're not. You live in a tiny house in a tiny town. No one cares what some queen says about your family."

He turns to Ella and frowns.

"A yellow dress? I thought you'd be Cinderella, too," he says. "Right? Cinder. Ella."

Then he hands back my apple with two big bites in it. No way am I it now.

He turns to leave. Kendra steps in front of him and makes him stop. "Why are you so mean?" she asks. "What did we do to you?"

Lucas just laughs and reaches towards her, trying to pull the tiara off her head. She gasps and smacks his hand away.

"Don't touch me!" she says. "You're so rude."

"I'm not mean. And I'm not rude. I just tell the truth," he says.

Just then, Mrs. Williams walks over and asks us if there is a problem.

Lucas shakes his head, but Ella speaks up first. "Yes, there is a problem!" she says, pointing at Lucas. "He's being rude and making fun of our costumes."

Mrs. Williams puts her hand on Lucas's shoulder and tells him that it's time to take a walk. I have a feeling they'll be looking for the principal.

We watch them walk out of the gym, then turn to each other. What should we do now? We were having fun before Lucas came up to us. He's so good at making me feel bad.

"Ignore him. He's just jealous," says Emily. "I came here to have fun and get candy. Let's keep going!"

We leave the gym and walk down to Mrs. Henry's room. She's dressed like the Magic School Bus teacher! She's wearing the fish- and starfish-themed dress from my favorite book, the one where her class dives to the bottom of the ocean. I knew Mrs. Henry would have a great outfit.

Her husband comes out of the classroom with more candy. He's wearing a wetsuit and carrying a cardboard, surfboard-shaped Magic School Bus.

Mr. Henry pretends to jump in surprise when he sees us, then drops into a deep bow.

"Princesses!" he says. "How wonderful. My ladies, has this party been to your satisfaction? Could I get you a cup of tea, or would you prefer bags of gummy worms?"

We giggle again, our argument with Lucas almost forgotten.

We take the gummy worms and keep moving down the hall, seeing each of our friend's teachers and even getting candy from our old kindergarten teacher.

When Mr. Andrew comes floating down the hall, he hands us each a full-size bar of candy. He says coordinating with his family's costume calls for an extra treat.

The best treat of all comes from Mrs. Palette. Our art teacher is standing outside of her classroom handing out art kits. We each get a "draw your own monster" kit with a cardboard monster cutout, crayons, and colorful googly eyes. My kit came with five pink, glittery eyes. Awesome! I can't wait to create my five-eyed monster.

That night I lay in bed, my head spinning with excitement and sugar. As I drift off to sleep, my mind wanders to what Lucas said. I can't believe he's so mean!

I can't believe we're both running for class president.

7. Destroyed

The next few days go by slowly. After eating so much candy last weekend, I need another sugar high. Schools should hand out bags of candy after Halloween to keep our energy levels up.

Lucas is still being mean, but now that Halloween is over, he doesn't have much to tease us about. All I have to do now is face him in tomorrow's election assembly. The fourth grade classes take turns voting tomorrow and Friday.

I'm still trying to finish my assembly speech,

but I'm also thinking about art class! We get to take home last week's project today. I can't wait to see what our projects look like now that they've dried.

When we line up outside of Mrs. Palette's classroom, the door is propped open and she's holding a broom – just like last week, when we found her cleaning up a big mess. There's a small pile of cookies, crackers and crumbs swept into a pile near her feet.

She reaches for the dustpan and gives us a sad smile.

"Come in!" she says. "Let me finish cleaning up this mess. Then we need to talk."

It's never a good sign when an adult says, "We need to talk." What happened to her classroom again? Why does she need to talk to *us* about it?

She finishes sweeping up the crumbs, then dumps them into the trash can. I see a few fish-shaped crackers fall into the trash with the rest of the crumbs.

Then Mrs. Palette sits down and sighs.

"You all know my art room was vandalized last week. Someone came into the room before class started and destroyed most of my materials. I'd really hoped it was a one-time thing," she says. "As you can see, it's happened again. Only this time, whoever came into my room didn't just mess with paint and a few boxes of food. They destroyed a few finished projects."

We all start whispering. Who would do this?

She gives our class a stern look, and we stop talking.

"I'd like to think that none of you would ruin school property. You know better than to touch another student's artwork. But is there anything you would like to tell me?"

We look at each other nervously. I start wondering who would do this. It's one thing to not like art, but why would you ruin someone's project that they worked so hard on?

After a minute of silence, Mrs. Palette stands up.

"If you'd like to speak to me privately, please see me after class. Tell a teacher if you see or hear anything about this," she says. "This needs to stop!"

She opens the closet where last week's projects were drying. It doesn't take much effort. The door doesn't latch well and it's always opened easily.

She pauses as she reaches for the first project, and reminds us that a few things were damaged. Then she calls out our names. One by one, we go to get our finished work.

Emily gets her palace back. It looks like it's still in one piece. I'm so happy for her! She really wanted to show her mom her work.

Jay's gum ball machine is missing a few gum balls. I'm not surprised. We had enough trouble getting them to stick in the first place. It wouldn't take a lot for it to fall apart.

Mrs. Palette gives him a few extra gum balls, and points to the super glue bottle on her desk. He sticks the missing balls back on his project and puts it back on the shelf. It should be dry by the end of the day, she tells him.

Then she pulls out a piece of white paper with a familiar blue fish bowl.

The castle is still there, because I drew it using colored pencils. But every one of my "fish" are gone! There are even holes in the paper, like each one was ripped off.

"I'm sorry, Paige. I know how much you enjoyed making this," she says. "We don't have time to fix this or make a new fish bowl in class, but I'll send some materials home if you'd like to make it again."

She hands me new pieces of thick paper and a small bag of fish-shaped crackers. I go back to my desk, trying not to look upset. This isn't fair! Why would someone ruin my project? My brother Franky would've loved my fish bowl. I was going to let him hang it in his room.

Now I'll have to make the whole thing again.

This isn't going to keep me angry, though. I need to stay focused on this week's election and tomorrow's assembly. Maybe Franky can help me make a new fish bowl. I'm sure he'd have more fun gluing everything together, instead of just hanging it on his wall.

When we all get back to class, even Mrs. Henry can't stop talking about what happened. Was it a prank? It wasn't a very funny prank, if that's the case. Or was it an animal? We learned at the farm that some animals are foragers and will eat almost anything.

Maybe there's a rat loose in the school. But why would he eat my crackers and not Emily's cookies? It looks like something, or someone, went straight for my project and barely touched the others.

Lucas walks past me, rolling his eyes. Maybe I do smell a rat. (Dad says that means something is suspicious.) It seems very suspicious that only my project was destroyed.

Could Lucas be causing trouble just to get himself elected class president?

8. Speech

I rush through my homework that night. I'll need extra time to finish my notes and speech.

That's right, a speech. Every student running for president has to give a five minute speech and answer questions from the other kids in their grade. The kids running for president can ask each other questions, too. I'm a little nervous about what questions Lucas will ask. He seems determined to make me look dumb.

With all these thoughts swirling around in my head, I've had a lot of trouble finishing my speech. But now the assembly is tomorrow, and Emily is coming over tonight to go over our plan. There's no time left to worry! I need to get this done.

I walk downstairs and find Dad at the kitchen table. He's reading the newspaper, which is a good sign. That means he didn't bring home too much homework. Teachers have homework, too. When I tell him that I'm having trouble finishing my speech and notes, he gives me a thoughtful look.

"Sit down. Tell me what you have so far," he says.

After listening to my art-in-the-classroom proposal again (I've talked about it a lot!), he smiles.

"You did a great job of explaining your platform," he says.

"What's a platform?" I ask. I imagine myself building a train station platform and begging the entire fourth grade class to ride my train, not Lucas's.

"A platform is another word for your ideas. It's your goals, and what you hope to get done," he says. "You need to tell your class why you'd make the best president. You've been working with Mrs. Palette, right? Make sure you give specific examples of what might happen in the classroom, and tell your classmates that you're working with teachers to make this actually happen."

As I write down some examples of how I'd like art used for teaching, Dad looks over my shoulder and offers suggestions.

The doorbell rings as we're finishing my list. Emily is here!

Emily wants people to know that if they vote for us, we'll get a lot done. She has her own ideas about what she'd like to see changed, but she also likes my idea of bringing art into the classroom.

Her job was to find a way to pay for art supplies, and she was talking to a few people this afternoon who might help us. She doesn't look very happy as she walks through our door.

"No luck," she says. "I talked to the principal and the school board. They loved the idea, but there isn't any money to pay for something this big. We'll have to figure it out on our own."

My heart sinks. Buying art supplies for one person isn't a big deal. Buying supplies for an entire school, or even just fourth grade, is a huge deal. We'd hoped the school would support us and give money to make this work.

It was such a great idea. I was so excited about it. There has to be a way to make this work!

Then I remember that Alex started on his own, with almost no money. His first step was convincing companies that his ideas were worth raising money for.

"I know what we can try," I say. "We just

need to make a few phone calls."

* * *

As my classmates start climbing into the gym bleachers for Thursday's election assembly, I carefully check my posters. I'm ready with two art projects that show how we can use art to learn math, reading, and more!

It's not time to share my posters yet, though. Lucas gets to give his speech first.

It's hard to watch Lucas's speech. It's pretty obvious that Dad gave me some great advice: Set clear goals, and figure out how to make them happen.

Lucas is making promises that I know he can't keep. He promises a free, all-you-can-eat ice cream buffet every Friday, and snacks in the classroom every morning. He tells kids that as class president, he'll also ban homework for fourth graders.

I see Mr. Andrew's eyebrows raise. He doesn't look too happy about the no-homework promise.

When another fourth grader asks how much it will cost to buy a snack in the morning, Lucas just shrugs. He says he's sure that the school will pay for it, because we deserve it.

At that point, Mr. Andrew steps forward and reminds us that any promises we make must be reasonable and approved by the school. He doesn't address Lucas directly, but I can tell he's talking to him.

Lucas sighs dramatically. "I still think these are great ideas," he says. "I'd work really hard to get us ice cream and no homework."

His friends clap enthusiastically as he sits down. The rest of us clap too, but not nearly as loud.

Now it's my turn. I try not to let anyone see

how nervous I am, and hold my head high as I walk to the front of the bleachers. I can do this!

I start by asking our classmates if they want learning to be more fun and hands-on. A few kids raise their hands and look interested. Becoming more confident, I start to explain how art helps me think differently and work through problems. A few more kids and even the teachers start nodding their heads.

Then I hold up my first poster board. It's pretty fun, if you ask me! I drew a person from head to toe, using fractions and a ruler to show how big a person's head, arms and legs should be compared to the rest of their body. It uses math, science and art to show how every person's body is perfectly proportioned.

"I've been working with Mrs. Palette on some ideas," I add. "We could set up an art learning station for each fourth grade classroom once a week. It would be a fun way to break things up and learn in new ways."

I flip to the next poster board. I took a few photos using my dad's old camera, and then wrote a short story about what I saw in the pictures.

It started as a few photos of my brother Franky jumping in puddles. Then I followed him to the park, where he found more puddles. I also took a picture of his wet footprints on the sidewalk.

Then I turned the photos into a story about a boy who likes to splash in puddles. He wanders away from home and gets lost. His mom finds him in the park after she follows his wet footprints!

I've never been a good writer, but it was almost easy once I made my story into an art project. Even though this was my idea, I'm still surprised by how well it worked.

My classmates seem impressed. I tell them

that I had a lot of fun making these projects, and know they would have fun too.

Most of the kids ask easy questions, but not Lucas. "Who's going to pay for this?" he asks. He still looks upset that the principal told him he couldn't promise a ton of fun things and expect the school to pay for it.

"I'm glad you asked!" I say. "As class president, I would find local sponsors to pay for some of our art supplies. I've also asked A+ Technology to work with our school. I've already contacted them and they spoke with Mrs. Palette last night. A+ will pay for an art teacher to help her. She's only one person, and having two art teachers would give both of them enough time to teach class *and* help our regular teachers bring their lessons to life through art."

I can't believe Alex came through for us! His company is A+ Technology, and he says that our ideas are a perfect fit for their new program.

They'll pay for one part-time teacher, plus our first month of art supplies, ten digital cameras and a photo printer. They'll even help us apply for grants to pay for the rest of the year.

The fourth graders clap as I sit down with my friends. They clap really loudly, which I think is a good sign!

Then Mr. Andrew asks the people running for vice president to come down to the gym floor. Emily and two boys climb down the bleacher steps.

The principal introduces each student, then reminds them that they may also give a short speech or presentation. The boys look surprised, but Emily is prepared.

Emily reminds everyone that she would work with A+ Technology to bring more money to our school. She also has a real plan for less homework. After talking to a few teachers, they've agreed that homework could be optional if you're getting good grades. Every student who earns an A for the week would get a week-long homework pass.

I'm proud of Emily. She's so smart, and really knows how to make good things happen!

When I call Alex that night, I'm still excited about our school's reaction. We may have a real chance to win this election.

"You both had some good ideas," he says. "Great job! You did your best. Now it's time for your classmates to vote."

Half of the classes voted today. The other half vote tomorrow. Then we'll hear the results in an assembly tomorrow afternoon.

9. On the Run

I'm nervous the day of the election. Butterflies flutter around my stomach, trying to find a way out. Whatever happens, I am determined to remain calm. Like a princess.

Princesses and queens aren't elected. They're born into their role. I may not become class president, but I *am* still a princess. I will find a way to change our school!

Lucas is not acting very prince-like today. I'm not sure why this surprises me. With just one hour until the last classes vote, he's still trying to discover who is destroying the art room. I guess he thinks that if he solves the mystery, we'll have to make him class president.

It's raining today. Instead of running around the playground, we're all stuck inside for morning recess. Lucas is using that time for some last-minute interrogating.

Walking down the hall, I see Lucas and Jay near their lockers. Lucas is asking Jay where he was last Monday. That's the day Mrs. Palette's room was first damaged.

"Can you prove that you got to school late that day?" Lucas demands, poking a finger into Jay's shoulder. "Let's see your late slip! If you were really late, the office gave you a late slip."

Jay's so scared that he's shaking. I can't help feeling bad for him. Jay loves Mrs. Palette. There's no way he would damage her classroom.

"I …. I … I was late, I really was!" Jay says. "I was looking for something and missed the bell.

I gave my late slip to Mrs. Henry!"

I stop in front of Lucas with my hands on my hips. "Leave Jay alone," I say. "He really was late that day. Remember? He almost missed computer class because he needed a late pass."

I shake my head and keep walking after Lucas lets Jay into his locker. Even if Lucas has good intentions, he's not being very kind. You can't march around the school accusing people. He's going to scare the rule breaker into a corner, where he (or she) will hide until we stop looking for them.

Maybe Lucas is doing us a favor. Maybe he really is scaring the person who did this. Maybe they'd be scared enough that we won't need to worry about any more drama.

With that thought, I walk towards the art classroom to check on Mrs. Palette. She might need some cheering up after such a rough week. And if there are any new clues, I want to be the first person to know about them. Solving this mystery won't help me win class president, but I really do care about Mrs. Palette and her classroom!

After nearly convincing myself that Lucas scared away any trouble, I'm surprised to see Mrs. Palette standing in her doorway. She looks shocked. What now?

She doesn't notice me for a minute, then seems surprised to see a student standing next to her.

"Paige! What are you doing here? I was just about to call the janitor," she says. "It looks like our trouble-maker is at it again. They've really outdone themselves this time."

She points towards the main table in her classroom. My jaw drops. Someone poured out all of the leftover boxes of macaroni, spaghetti and other kinds of pasta that Mrs. Palette used for our food-as-art projects.

There are 400 students at Riverview Elementary School, and every single one of them takes art class with Mrs. Palette. There was a lot of pasta.

The boxes were thrown in a trash can near the tables. What kind of vandal makes a mess, but also takes the time to clean part of that mess up?

The biggest mystery isn't hiding in the trash can, though. What really confuses me is what someone did with the noodles. They carefully shaped each pile into a letter, spelling out "HELP!"

"Mrs. Palette, who did this?" I ask. "Does someone really need our help?"

"I don't know. Probably not. There are better ways to ask for help than to spell it out in noodles," she points out.

She reaches for a dustpan and walks towards the letters, dragging the trash can behind her.

"Wait!" I yell. "Don't clean it up yet. We need

to document the evidence."

I walk around the room, taking pictures of the mess with her phone. Then I push the trash can towards the table and help her sweep every noodle into the trash.

It's such a waste. There are still a few classes who haven't done the food art project. What will those kids use now? I guess they'll have to use cookies, crackers and gum balls instead.

After helping Mrs. Palette clean up, recess time is almost over. I walk slowly back to our classroom. My brain is ready to explode with questions.

I'm so lost in my thoughts that I almost walk into Jay. He's still in the hallway and sitting next to his locker. When he turns to look at me, his face is covered in tears.

"Jay! What's wrong?" I ask. "It's not Lucas, is it? He's not worth being this upset."

I sit down on the cold tile floor, and slide

closer to him. Jay wipes the tears from his face and laughs. Then he looks around our hallway, like he's making sure no one else can hear us.

"I can handle Lucas. He's all talk," Jay says. "But can you keep a secret? I think I might be in trouble."

"Of course I can keep a secret! What's wrong?" I ask again. "What can I do to help? Should I get Mrs. Henry?"

"No!" he whispers loudly. "Don't get Mrs. Henry. I don't want anyone to know. It's just that … I didn't mean to. But I think it's my fault that Mrs. Palette's room is being messed up. And now I don't know what to do."

Jay's fault? There's no way Jay would damage someone else's stuff. Would he? I'm hurt, angry, and confused. I take a deep breath, try to stay calm, and ask him what he means.

"I didn't want to tell anyone. Remember when I was late last week? I got to school on time, but lost my pet mouse on the way to homeroom. He jumped right out of his cage when the cage door popped open!" Jay says. "I was bringing him for Show and Tell. I didn't want to get in trouble. I've been trying to catch him for more than a week. I put his favorite treats in my locker, and they're gone every night …"

"And you think he's still in the school, eating the food in the art room?" I finish for him. "Oh no, Jay!"

"Yeah," he sighs. "I wanted to tell someone, but I've been afraid to. Lucas really wants to get someone in trouble for this. I was afraid to tell anyone after waiting this long."

I sit quietly and think. Who should we go to for help?

Mr. Andrew has always been fair to us, even when we don't exactly follow the rules. I think the principal will be able to help. I convince Jay to come with me to Mr. Andrew's office to tell the whole story. Maybe Mr. Andrew can even help us catch Jay's pet.

We walk to his office and wait to talk to Mr. Andrew.

One thing still bothers me, though. Who spelled "help?" in the art classroom?

10. Mystery Solved

Mr. Andrew comes out of his office and gives us a big smile.

"Come in!" he says. "What brings you here today? I'm sorry to tell you this, but I don't have any more candy bars."

He laughs at his own joke, and we smile half-heartedly. We sit at the round table next to Mr. Andrew's desk after he closes the door.

I look at Jay. He looks back at me with wide eyes.

"I… I… I have to tell you …." Jay stutters.

He stops talking and stares at the table.

Mr. Andrew stops smiling and sits down. "You haven't been a student here for very long, but I tell every student that my office is a safe place," he says. "Even if you've done something wrong, the best thing to do is talk to me. We can work together to make it right."

Jay sighs. He twirls his finger around the strings on his jacket, then looks at me and asks, "Will you tell him?"

I nod. "Mr. Andrew, Jay didn't mean to do it. But we know who is making a mess in Mrs. Palette's room."

Mr. Andrew raises his eyebrows. I take a deep breath and continue, telling him everything that I know. Jay's pet mouse has been loose in the school for nearly two weeks. We think he might be the reason there's food being pulled out of storage closets and damage to the food art. And while Jay's tried to catch his pet, he hasn't been able to.

"He's really sorry," I say. "He just needs help to catch…. Jay, what's your mouse's name?"

"Mini," Jay whispers. "His name is Mini. And his favorite food is cheese. I've been trying to catch him with cheese crackers all week, but he's just eating the snacks and disappearing. And I've been wanting to tell someone for days that he was probably making the mess, but I was afraid."

Jay sits a bit taller and looks Mr. Andrew in the eyes, looking braver.

"I'm really sorry, Mr. Andrew! I can't believe I lost him. And I'd like some help getting him back," he says.

Mr. Andrew looks at him seriously.

"This is a big problem, but thank you for coming to tell me," he says. "There won't be a punishment this time, but I do want you to apologize to your classmates for the damage Mini has done. From now on, you must tell a teacher or myself right away if you need help."

Jay nods eagerly.

"Oh, I will!" he says. "I've been so worried Mini would get hurt, but I was even more worried I would get kicked out of school."

"Kicked out of school?" Mr. Andrew laughs. "No way. If you had come to me sooner, we could have helped you catch Mini a week ago. Less worry for you, and less mess for Mrs. Palette."

We all stand up and move towards the door. The principal tells his assistant that he needs to take a walk with us, then calls the janitor to ask for his help. The janitor is the first person in the building every morning, and we think Mini was exploring the school overnight and in the mornings, so he's the perfect person to help us.

"So tell me," Mr. Andrew says as we leave the main office. "You named your pet Mini Mouse?"

I giggle. It's a cute name.

"It was my sister's idea!" Jay says. "He was the smallest mouse at the pet store."

First we go upstairs to Mrs. Palette's room. She's busy filling the display cabinet with paper pumpkins. Not jack 'o lanterns, of course. Now that Halloween is over, it's time to make Thanksgiving crafts. She probably thinks it's safer to use paper pumpkins, instead of real pumpkins that might get smashed or nibbled.

Jay apologizes and explains what's been going on. For some reason, she doesn't look surprised. Maybe she already guessed it was an animal because of the empty food boxes.

"But Mr. Andrew! Mrs. Palette!" I say, suddenly remembering. "Who was writing 'help'? It couldn't have been Mini!"

Mrs. Palette tries to hide a smile. Does she know something that we don't know?

"I'm sure we'll figure that out too," she says. "Jay, thank you for being honest. You can help me clean up the rest of this mess later. I've still got a lot of organizing to do."

Jay agrees to stay after school to help her, and we walk down the stairs to Mrs. Henry's room. Our teacher isn't in the room yet, but Mr. Andrew stays in the room while Jay apologizes to his classmates for the damage Mini did to our art projects. Then the principal comes to stand next to Jay and smiles.

"Now that we know what happened to the food in Mrs. Palette's room, we need your help!" he says. "Has anyone seen or heard something that might be a mouse? We'll need to work together to get Mini back."

When no one says anything, he asks us all to keep our eyes and ears open for clues. Mr. Andrew pats Jay on his shoulder and promises to share any news of Mini. But as he reaches for the doorknob to leave the classroom, the door opens.

In walks Mr. Reese, the school janitor. He's holding a small cardboard box.

"I found something this morning. Were you looking for this?" he asks Mr. Andrew, handing him the box.

Mr. Andrew peeks into the box.

"What a great surprise!" he says. "Jay, you need to see this."

Jay cheers with delight as a small, chocolate-colored mouse peaks its head out of the box.

"Mini!" he says. "Mr. Reese, you found him!"

"I caught him overnight using some snacks I found in an open locker. I guess you've been leaving your locker door open, hoping to catch him?" he asks. "It was a good idea. But you needed a better cage, one that he couldn't get out of after he ate the treat."

He leans over and pretends to examine Mini. I hear him tell Jay softly, "Sometimes it's OK to ask for an adult's help, especially when you have a problem that's taking over the whole school. He could have hurt himself. A school is not a safe place for a pet mouse."

Mr. Reese stands up and waves to the rest of the class, then turns to go out the door.

"Wait!" I yell to him. "Mr. Reese, there's still one mystery left. Who wrote 'help' in the art room?"

The janitor grins, looking a little bit sheepish.

"Well, that was me," he admits. "It gets too quiet when I'm the only person in the building. I thought I'd be the one cleaning up the mess anyway, so I took the noodles that were spilled on the table and had some fun."

We all laugh. Even though I ended up helping Mrs. Palette clean up the noodles, I can't be mad. It was a funny thing to do.

Mr. Andrew takes Mini and promises to keep him safe until school is over. The moment they're out the door, Lucas jumps to his feet.

"I knew it was an animal!" shouts Lucas. "There was no way a person would make that kind of mess. And I knew Jay was acting suspicious, too. See, I solved the mystery!"

Jay rolls his eyes. "The janitor solved the mystery," he says. "And Paige convinced me to tell the teachers what was happening before we talked to the janitor. She was way nicer than you were, too."

Lucas's face turns bright red. But before he can say one word, Mrs. Henry rushes into the room.

"Sorry I'm late, everyone! There's no time to start our math lesson. Let's go vote," she says.

11. Princess for President

My heart pounds as we walk down the hallway to the cafeteria. That's where every class is voting for their new class officers.

I'm nervous about voting. What if I don't win? What if I *do* win? Would I be a good class president?

As we walk into the cafeteria, my eyes are drawn to the five voting booths set up against the back wall. They're the same voting booths we used last year in third grade – a three-sided square just big enough to fit one desk, with back and side walls. There's a dark blue curtain covering the front of each booth.

I stand in line with the rest of my classmates. When it's my turn, Mrs. Henry hands me a piece of paper and points towards an empty voting booth. I take a deep breath and push aside the blue curtain, and step inside.

The paper lists the students running for each office in fourth grade, with instructions to choose one student for each office. I circle my own name for class president, of course. Even the President of the United States gets a chance to vote for themselves! Then I circle Emily's name for vice president.

For secretary, I circle Peyton Brown's name. I haven't had class with Peyton since we were in first grade, but I liked working with him. I pick Brook Miller for treasurer. She is smart and had some good ideas for fundraisers.

I fold my voting sheet in half and slide it

through the slot in the back of the voting booth. There's soft thump as it hits the other pieces of paper in a box outside our booth.

When I push back the curtain, I feel better. I've done the best that I could over the past two weeks. I still hope that I win. But I'm also happy that we solved the mystery in Mrs. Palette's room. I didn't need to be class president to help Mrs. Palette or Jay.

I didn't need to be a princess to help them, either.

I can make a big difference as class president. But now I know that I can make a difference even if I'm just me.

Jay gives me a shy smile as I walk towards him and Emily. The cafeteria is almost empty. It looks like we were one of the last classes to vote.

There's nothing left to do but wait. The PTO will finish counting votes soon, and Mr. Andrew will announce the new class officers during an assembly at the end of the day.

Mrs. Henry tries to start our math lesson when we get back, but between the election, solving Mrs. Palette's mystery, and finding Mini, we're all distracted. It's been a crazy day!

After a short lesson, Mrs. Henry announces that it's STEAM time.

I love STEAM time. Our teacher calls it "blowing off steam time" because we can play and learn when our brains are just too foggy to focus. STEAM stands for science, technology, engineering, art and math. It's a lot of fun. I love having free time to work with art supplies, building blocks and the coding robot she has in her room.

Our coding robot is a mouse. Emily, Jay and I grab the mouse and find a corner in the back of the room. We spend the next 30 minutes giving the robot instructions to go through a tunnel, dodge a wall, and find a piece of fake cheese.

Jay laughs when we finally get it right. The mouse gives a loud squeak and plays some music when its nose hits the cheese.

"That's the same noise Mini makes when he finds his favorite snacks," he says. "I really am sorry about last week, Paige. His favorite food is cheddar crackers, so your fish bowl didn't stand a chance."

Mini has excellent taste. That's my favorite snack too!

"It's OK, Jay. My little brother had fun making a new fish bowl," I say. "And then we ate the rest of the crackers! My dad thinks it's funny that we like pink princess crackers so much."

We put the coding robot back on the shelf and grab some colored pencils and paper. The three of us doodle until Mrs. Henry announces that it's time to get ready for the assembly. I glance down at my paper. Not bad. I drew a mermaid surrounded by pink cheddar crackers, with a tiny golden castle in the background. There's a pirate ship sailing above her on the choppy ocean waves.

Emily drew a heart. At least, I'm pretty sure it's a heart. It's got veins and arteries and everything! It would make a great art-science lesson. The rest of her paper is filled with cute emoji hearts.

Jay's drawing a block of Swiss cheese next to a little brown mouse. I'm pretty sure he's still thinking about Mini.

We put our art supplies back on the STEAM shelf and line up with our classmates. We walk to the auditorium, the only room big enough for all of the students and teachers.

Once the entire school is settled into rows and rows of seats, Mr. Andrew climbs the steps to stand on the stage.

"Good afternoon!" he says. "This is a very exciting day. Our PTO volunteers have spent the last two days counting votes, and it's time to announce this year's class officers!"

He starts clapping, and the rest of us join him.

"As you know, every class from first through sixth grade has a chance to elect their own president, vice president, secretary and treasurer. They have the important job of working with our teachers to make their classmates' voices heard, and to help find solutions for problems they see in the school," says Mr. Andrew.

He makes a big show of opening an envelope with "First Grade" written on the front, then announces the newest president of the first grade class. A tiny girl with a high ponytail stands up and grins while her classmates clap, and Mr. Andrew invites her to come up on stage with him. The rest of the first grade officers are soon lined up next to her.

Next comes second and third grade. I know a few kids in the grades below me, but still don't recognize any of the class officers.

Finally, Mr. Andrew pulls out an envelope marked "Fourth Grade" from the podium on stage. This is it!

"The new class president for fourth grade is …" Mr. Andrew pauses. "Paige Johnson! Paige, come up here, please!"

If I thought my heart was pounding when we voted, it's pumping even harder now! I carefully climb the steps to the auditorium stage and shake Mr. Andrew's hand.

I clap the loudest of all my classmates when Emily becomes our vice president. I'm just as excited when Brook comes to the stage as our new treasurer. Three girls! None of the other classes have three girls as their class officers.

When Mr. Andrew calls Peyton's name for secretary, I still smile. It would have been nice to have an all-girl team, but Peyton was always a hard worker. He'll be fun to work with.

Peyton walks to the front of the auditorium and stands next to Emily, Brook and me. We turn to each other and smile, then walk off of the stage and sit together with the other officers. I can feel my excitement growing. We are going to make an amazing team!

We wait while the fifth and sixth grade class officers are announced, then watch the rest of the school slowly walk out of the auditorium and back to their homerooms. There are just a few minutes until the bell rings for the end of the day, but Mr. Andrew asks to speak to us before we leave.

After the last student leaves and the auditorium doors fall shut, Mr. Andrew comes to stand in front of us.

"What a great group of kids!" he says to us. "Each of you has a very important job for this year. Can anyone tell me what that job is?"

A fifth grader raises her hand confidently.

"We work together to make the school a better place," she says. "That's what you told us last year."

"Yes, that's right," says Mr. Andrew. "But more importantly, this year I have a new job for you. I want you to listen. Listen to your classmates. Listen to your teachers. What do they want, what are their concerns? You are some of the brightest students in this school. Your job is to listen and think about how we can make this school the best it can be!"

We all nod.

I can't wait to see what the rest of this year brings.

AUTHOR'S NOTE

I hope you enjoyed the second Princess Paige book!
I had so much fun watching Paige figure out what it means to be a princess – and learning that sometimes, even a regular girl can do big things.

If you enjoyed this book, please ask an adult to help you leave a review on Amazon. Reviews are the BEST way to say "thank you!" to an author.

Special thanks to my first readers, including Quinn, Jan, Kylee, Zoe, and Beth. Your encouragement means the world to me. Thank you for sharing everything that you love about Princess Paige, and for your amazing eyes that find my last-minute mistakes.

ABOUT THE AUTHOR

Stacey Solt is the author of the Princess Paige series. She was born and raised in eastern Pennsylvania, where she lives with her husband and two children.

Stacey never outgrew her love of children's books. When she's not reading or writing, Stacey enjoys spending time outdoors. She's happiest at the beach — but watching a beautiful sunset from her porch at home makes her pretty happy, too.

Princess Paige

QUEEN OF HEARTS

Turn the page for more of
Princess Paige's adventures!

1. Heart Month

My name is Paige Johnson. I am in fourth grade at Riverview Elementary School.

I discovered that I'm a princess a few months ago. My great-grandfather was a prince from Altura before he moved to America as a little boy. Being a princess hasn't changed my life much, but I've learned that you don't need to be a princess to make big changes in the world.

Today is the first day of February. There's so much to do this month!

As the fourth grade class president, I'm on the Valentine's Day dance committee. We're in charge of the food and music, and we'll decorate the gym before the dance.

My birthday is also in February. I'll turn ten years old on February 10, and my birthday party is next week. We'll probably have a heart theme again. I love hearts.

That brings me to my favorite thing about February. February is heart month! We celebrate by sending valentines this month, but it's also time to think about heart health. My friend Hailey O'Connor knows a lot about heart health. She had heart surgery as a baby and is helping our school celebrate heart month.

Hailey isn't in my class this year, but everyone in fourth grade is going to see her right now. We're going to the gym to hear Hailey talk. We'll also watch a video about her! I'm so excited to see Hailey's video.

Our teacher, Mrs. Henry, leads us to the gym. We climb up the bleachers and I sit behind Ms. Martha's class with Emily Ellis, my best friend.

As I look around the room, I see a few of my friends from other classes. I turn and wave to Kendra Kelly, who waves back with a huge grin. She's friends with Hailey, too.

Hailey is standing at the front of the gym, talking to a tall woman in a dark suit. Once all of fourth grade is sitting in the bleachers, the tall woman steps forward and smiles at us.

"Good morning!" she says. "My name is Mrs. Mitchell. I'm from the American Heart Association. I'm here to talk about heart month. But first I want to introduce my special guest."

She looks back at Hailey, who waves at all of us. Hailey gives me a big grin when Emily and I start cheering.

"Hailey O'Connor is here to help us start heart month at Riverview Elementary. She is one of our state ambassadors for the American Heart Association, but she is also a student at Riverview! Today we're going to talk about heart month and see the video that we made with Hailey's help. Lights, please?" she asks, looking at the principal standing near the light switch. Mr. Andrew nods and turns to dim the lights.

As the lights dim, a screen drops slowly from the gym ceiling. The screen shines brightly with the American Heart Association's symbol.

Suddenly the picture changes. It's Hailey, on the giant screen!

"Hello, my name is Hailey O'Connor. I had heart surgery when I was two months old," she says in the video.

The picture changes to a video of her in gymnastics class. First, we see her flying between the uneven bars, graceful and beautiful. Then the camera cuts to her doing a back handspring during her floor routine.

Hailey is in my gymnastics class. It's easy to forget that she has heart problems when you see her on the floor. She's strong, and she's fast.

She's on our competition team and one of the best athletes at the gym.

Hailey comes back on the screen to tell us that the American Heart Association raises millions of dollars for heart research every year.

"I was born with Tetralogy of Fallot, a congenital heart defect that meant my heart didn't pump blood correctly from my lungs to my body. I needed surgery to survive. And I'm not alone," she said. "Heart defects are the most common type of birth defect. One in 110 babies born each year will have some type of heart defect."

She thanked the American Heart Association for continuing research that will help kids and adults with heart problems, and ended the video by encouraging us all to take care of our hearts.

The screen dims, and the lights in the gym turn back on.

Mrs. Mitchell puts her hand on Hailey's shoulder.

"Thank you, Hailey! You did a great job, and we're proud to have you on the American Heart Association's team," she says, turning to address the rest of us. "Like Hailey said, heart health is so important. It's not something only adults need to worry about. Kids can have heart problems, too. But even if you're born with a perfect heart, you still need to take care of it! You need to exercise, and eat right, and make sure that your heart stays healthy for your entire life."

Mrs. Mitchell walks to the bleachers and picks up a stack of folders. As she talks, Hailey hands a folder to each teacher.

"A big part of the American Heart Association's mission is to raise money for heart research and education," says Mrs. Mitchell. "Riverview Elementary will be raising money this month by having a jump rope marathon! We're going to practice jumping rope today, and I'm also giving each of your teachers a sponsor form. You can ask people to sponsor you during our marathon and raise money for heart health."

Our gym teacher, Mrs. Walck, steps forward with a big box. The box is filled to the top with jump ropes.

"OK, kids," she shouts. "We're going to wrap up our assembly with a little exercise! There are plenty of jump ropes to share. Let's break into groups and take turns jumping rope as long as you can. Who can do the most jumps without stopping?"

As everyone climbs down the bleachers, Emily, Kendra and I rush towards Hailey. Kendra walks over to the gym teacher to get a jump rope.

"How'd I do?" Hailey asks while we wait. "I was so nervous. This was my first time seeing the video, and I'll be going to more schools with Mrs. Mitchell next week."

"You did great!" I assure her. "Mrs. Mitchell is lucky to have you."

Kendra walks back to us, gently swinging the jump rope at her side.

"I'm feeling pretty energetic today," she says. "I bet I can jump at least thirty times. Can anyone beat that?"

"You're on, Kendra," says Hailey. "I can do at least forty jumps."

Kendra starts jumping over the rope, counting to ten, twenty, thirty. She counts thirty-five jumps before she finally stumbles on the rope.

"Beat that!" she says, wiggling her eyebrows. "We're not going to take it easy on you just because it's heart month. Show us what you've got!"

Hailey laughs and takes the rope from her friend. She jumps over the rope, counting to ten, twenty… but by the time she counts to twenty-five, she's breathing hard.

She trips on the rope and nearly falls into me. "Sorry, sorry," she says. "I didn't sleep last night, and I'm really tired today. Maybe I was too excited."

Hailey is never tired. I've seen her spend hours practicing her gymnastics routine, and she's always moving when she's not sitting in class. But we're all allowed to have bad days, right? After catching her breath, she hands me the jump rope and tells me to beat Kendra.

I do it, too. I jump over the rope forty-three times. Just as I'm handing the rope to Emily, Mrs. Walck calls for everyone to stop. It's time to get back to class.

I can't wait to see what else we do during heart month.

Made in United States
Troutdale, OR
02/26/2024

17995165R00083